THE FLYING BEAVER BROTHERS
BIRDS VS. BUNNIES

MAXWELL EATON III

ALFRED A. KNOPF
NEW YORK

THIS IS
A BORZOI
BOOK
PUBLISHED BY
ALFRED A. KNOPF

This is a work of fiction. Names, characters, places, and incidents either are the product of the author's imagination or are used fictitiously. Any resemblance to actual persons, living or dead, events, or locales is entirely coincidental.

Copyright © 2013 by Maxwell Eaton III

All rights reserved. Published in the United States by Alfred A. Knopf, an imprint of Random House Children's Books, a division of Random House, Inc., New York.

Knopf, Borzoi Books, and the colophon are registered trademarks of Random House, Inc.

Visit us on the Web! randomhouse.com/kids
Educators and librarians, for a variety of teaching tools, visit us at RHTeachersLibrarians.com

Library of Congress Cataloging-in-Publication Data
Eaton, Maxwell.
The flying beaver brothers : birds vs. bunnies /
Maxwell Eaton III. — 1st ed.
    p.   cm.
Summary: Ace and Bub's plans for a quiet vacation are put on hold when they are stranded on an island where their nemesis, Walter, has stirred up trouble between the birds and the rabbits
ISBN 978-0-449-81022-4 (trade) — ISBN 978-0-449-81023-1 (lib. bdg.) —
ISBN 978-0-449-81024-8 (ebook)
[1. Graphic novels. 2. Beavers—Fiction. 3. Islands—Fiction.
4. Rabbits—Fiction. 5. Birds—Fiction.] I. Title.
PZ7.7.E18Flb 2013
741.5'973—dc23
2012034047

The illustrations in this book were created using pen and ink with digital coloring.

MANUFACTURED IN MALAYSIA
July 2013
10 9 8 7 6 5 4 3 2 1
First Edition

Random House Children's Books supports the First Amendment and celebrates the right to read.

FOR KEE

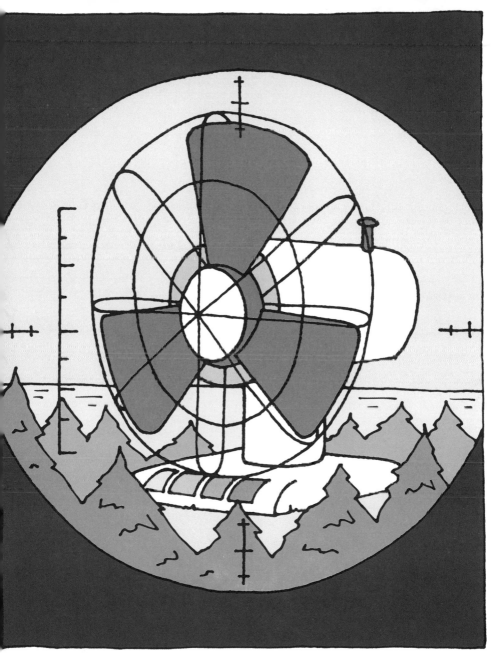

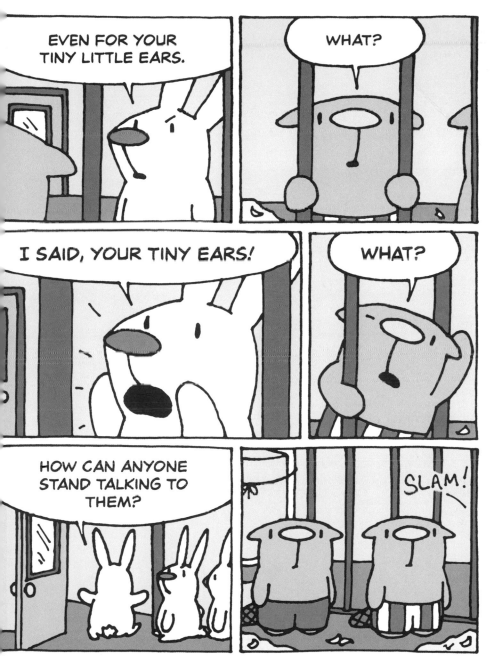

THIS COULDN'T HAVE WAITED UNTIL MORNING?

HEY, WHERE DID HE GO?

RIGHT HERE. FOLLOW ME.

WELCOME.

WHAT IS THIS PLACE?

OUR HOME EVER SINCE THE *BUNNY* PROBLEM BEGAN.

BUNNY PROBLEM?

YOU SEE, THE BUNNIES ARE TRYING TO KICK US OFF THE ISLAND.

THEY EVEN BUILT A GIANT WIND-MAKING MACHINE TO BLOW US OUT OF THE SKY!

YEAH, WE HEARD. . . .

SO WE MOVED INTO THIS CANYON, WHERE WE WERE SAFE FROM THE WIND-MAKER.

OF COURSE, WE NEEDED A WAY TO DEFEND OURSELVES.

OF COURSE.

AND THAT'S WHERE OUR GOOD FRIEND WALLY CAME IN. . . .

WALLY?!

WALTER MACKEREL THE FOURTH?!

SO WHAT ARE YOU DOING HERE?

WELL, MY LAST BUSINESS RAN INTO SOME TROUBLE . . .

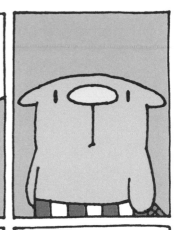

SO I CAME HERE TO DO SOME THINKING. SOME REFLECTING. TO GET AWAY FROM THE RAT RACE.

NO OFFENSE.

WE'RE ACTUALLY BEAVERS.

HUH.

SO THE ONLY ONE WHO KNOWS WHAT'S HAPPENING IS WALTER MACKEREL.

SSSH!

PROBABLY.

BUT ARE WE BEING TOO HARD ON HIM?

WE *DID* DESTROY HIS FACTORY. . . .

MAYBE HE REALLY IS HERE TO RELAX. MAYBE WALTER HAS CHANGED!

OR MAYBE HE HASN'T.

HEY, SQUIRRELS!
TIRED OF DEALING WIT
CARROT-GRUBBING BUNNIES
WELL, BUILD YOUR NEW HOME O
ACOR
A PARADISE FOR SQUIRRELS

UNCLE WALLY?

HE'S MAKING THEM FIGHT SO THAT HE CAN HAVE THE ISLAND ALL TO HIMSELF!

WITH THE BUNNIES UNDERGROUND AND THE BIRDS IN THE CANYON, HE CAN DO WHATEVER HE WANTS!

CLASSIC WALTER MACKEREL.

WE'D BETTER TELL THEM WHAT'S GOING ON AND PUT A STOP TO THIS FIGHT!

BUT THEY'RE GOING TO THINK WE'RE SPIES SINCE WE ESCAPED EACH OF THEM.

BACK AT THE NOISE-MAKER . . .

ONLY WALLY HELPS THE BUNNIES.

IT WAS WALLY WHO SENT ME! HE TOLD ME TO TELL YOU THAT THE BIRDS ARE DEFENSELESS.

YOU'RE TELLING ME THAT HE TOLD YOU TO TELL US THAT THE BIRDS ARE DEFENSELESS?

YOU'RE TELLING ME THAT YOU DON'T *BELIEVE* THAT HE TOLD ME TO TELL YOU?

WELL, WHETHER YOU'RE TELLING ME THAT HE TOLD YOU TO TELL US OR WHETHER YOU'RE JUST TELLING US AND HE DIDN'T TELL YOU SO THAT YOU'RE ACTUALLY JUST TELLING . . .